The Magic Mist

by Tony Lang
Illustrations by Helen Marshall

The Magic Mist

By the same author (under the pen-name of Lachlan Ness):

A Kangaroo Loose in the Top Paddock

A Kangaroo Loose in Shetland

One Memorable Summer – a Scottish Adventure

The Ness Fireside Book of God Ghosts Ghouls and other true stories

National Library of Australia Cataloguing-in-Publication entry

Author: Lang, Anthony D., author.
Other Authors/Contributors: Marshall, Helen G., illustrator.

Title: The magic mist / Tony Lang ; Helen Marshall, illustrator.

ISBN: 9780987408457 (paperback)

Target Audience: For primary school age.

Subjects: Animals--Australia--Juvenile poetry.
                     Fantasy poetry.

Dewey Number: A821.4

Published by Akangarooloose.com

Cover and illustrations by Helen Marshall
Printed by CreateSpace

The Magic Mist

I strolled into the bush one day-

What happened next is hard to say.

A fairy-mist the forest wreathed

And charmed the very air I breathed.

A magic aura touched each tree,

Each plant and creature - even me.

Beyond the normal world I knew,

A hidden earth had come to view.

Across my path marched lines of ants

In brightly coloured shoes and pants.

I knew that in the misty haze

Stranger sights would meet my gaze.

The next I saw - I swear it's true:

A bush hat on a kangaroo!

He gave a wave and smiled at me

(And that was odd enough to see),

But stranger still, I must relate,

He spoke to me: "How are you, mate?"

Then doffed his hat with practised ease

And bounded off among the trees.

I shook my head - my mind was numb.

I wondered what was yet to come.

And then before my very eyes

I had another great surprise.

Along a track I'd wandered down

A wombat in a dressing gown

Sat drinking tea and eating toast.

"Come, sit," he said, "I'll be your host."

He nodded to his table there

And to another, vacant chair.

I sat at once. The chair was small,

For wombats are not very tall.

We chatted on of this and that,

I spoke in English, he, Wombat.

And when at last I rose to go,

He waved the teapot to and fro.

"Just one more round of toast and tea

And then we can part company."

He shook my hand, I took his paw,

Then stayed another hour or more.

I wandered on, till wearied sank

On a billabong's grassy bank.

Just then I heard a gentle song

That floated from the billabong.

I was entranced! A golden carp

Sat playing on an Irish harp,

A sweet and mystic melody

Of life beneath her inland sea.

Cumbungi swayed and sang along

By that enchanted billabong.

"The song is lovely! I could stay

And listen to it all the day!"

I called to her. She heard it clear,

For in her eye I saw a tear.

"I can but stay for just a minute;

My air must have some water in it,

So take a willow, soft and fine,

And with it soothe my golden spine.

I do this every thousand years,

For weeping willows hold my tears."

I turned, and there upon the shore

A weeping willow tree I saw.

I took a branch, as I was told,

And with it soothed her spine of gold.

She sighed. "Your kindness I'll not spurn;

I'll give you something in return."

Then she was gone! The waters bland

Had swallowed her, but in my hand,

When I my fingers did uncurl,

Found there a lovely, golden pearl.

I wandered from that magic place

With slow and steady, lingering pace,

And every creature that I viewed

Was full of colour, brightly hued.

Birds flew round on silvered wing,

While bees could talk and trees could sing.

But suddenly, before my gaze

That world was gone; so was the haze.

The mystic place that I'd been shown

Was now the bush I'd always known.

Long years have passed, yet still I yearn

To see that magic world's return.

And on the bushland paths, always

I hope to see the mystic haze.

I saw a 'roo one day, and think

He passed me with a knowing wink.

Sometimes I wonder if I'm mad

Or if it was a dream I had,

But when those doubts begin to swirl,

I gaze upon my golden pearl.

Some words to think about

Here are some words from our story. See how many you know, and what they mean. If you are uncertain or don't know, see if you can discover their meanings. It will add to your enjoyment of this magical story.

Wreathed • aura • doffed • host • vacant • billabong • entranced • carp • cumbungi • spurn • bland • lingering • pace • hued • yearn

See if you can find any other words you may not know. Can you find out their meanings?

Use your imagination to colour the picture on the page opposite.

TONY LANG is an Australian writer with a love of all living creatures, and a heightened sense of the strange and mysterious. He lives with his wife Janet and their two "children", Tonkie the Tonkinese cat and Jock the border collie on the shores of Lake Macquarie NSW. (The two-legged children have all grown up and gone).

HELEN MARSHALL is an accomplished artist, illustrator and author. She lives on the shores of Lake Macquarie and finds inspiration from her beautiful surroundings.

She trained in graphic design, interior design and fine arts, and is very involved with her community. Book covers and illustrations take much of her time, but she always makes sure she has time to write. Her first novel p.u.l.s.e. is due for release in 2014.

Made in the USA
Charleston, SC
15 December 2014